JAMES STEVENSON

GREENWILLOW
BOOKS
NEW
YORK

Are We Almost There?

Printed in Hong Kong by
South China Printing Co.

First Edition   10 9 8 7 6 5 4 3 2 1

Library of Congress Cataloging in Publication Data

Stevenson, James, (date)
Are we almost there?
Summary: Two puppy brothers, fighting
on the way to the beach with their father,
must learn to get along with each other
to keep their trip from ending early.
1. Children's stories, American.
[1. Behavior—Fiction.
2. Dogs—Fiction] I. Title.
PZ7.S84748Ar 1985   [E]   84-25847
ISBN 0-688-04238-4
ISBN 0-688-04239-2 (lib. bdg.)

THAT WATER WAS WONDERFUL!
WHO WANTS ANOTHER SANDWICH?
MAYBE HALF.
LET'S BUILD A SAND CASTLE NOW!

WASHINGTON PUBLIC LIBRARY
WASHINGTON, NEW JERSEY

JE   J55909
Ste

Are We Almost There?